Violence in Public Places

Perspectives on Violence

by Gus Gedatus

Consultant:
Vikki L. Sanders
Workplace Violence Prevention Coordinator
Department of Labor and Industry/
Workplace Safety Consultation
St. Paul, Minnesota

LifeMatters
an imprint of Capstone Press
Mankato, Minnesota

LifeMatters Books are published by Capstone Press
PO Box 669 • 151 Good Counsel Drive • Mankato, Minnesota 56002
http://www.capstone-press.com

Printed in the United States of America

Library of Congress Cataloging-in-Publication Data
Gedatus, Gustav Mark.
Violence in public places / by Gus Gedatus.
p. cm. — (Perspectives on violence)
Includes bibliographical references and index.
Summary: Describes the history, forms, causes, and effects of violence in public places and discusses ways to prevent or live with such violence.
ISBN 0-7368-0428-5 (book) — 0-7368-0439-0 (series)
1. Violent crimes—United States—Juvenile literature. 2. Violence—United States—Juvenile literature. [1. Violence. 2. Violent crimes.] I. Title. II. Series.
HV6789.G43 2000
364.1—dc21 99-049848
CIP

Staff Credits
Charles Pederson, editor; Adam Lazar, designer; Jodi Theisen, photo researcher

Photo Credits
Cover: The Stock Market/©Michel Heron, large; PNI/©Bill Pierce, small
FPG International/©Michael Krasowitz, 16
International Stock/©Christopher Morris, 11; ©Scott Barrow, 30; ©Bill Stanton, 38
Photo Network/©Jeff Greenberg, 7; ©Tom McCarthy Photos, 21; ©David N. Davis, 27
Photri/39, 44; ©Skjold, 57
Unicorn/©Alon Reininger, 12; ©Novastock, 59
Uniphoto/36
Visuals Unlimited/©Jeff Greenberg, 35, 54

A 0 9 8 7 6 5 4 3 2 1

Table of Contents

Chapter Overview

Violent crime has been decreasing in both the United States and Canada.

A public place is anywhere people can legally gather.

Violence in public places might include vandalism or shouting between two people.

Robbery, assault, reckless manslaughter, random violence, hate crimes, and terrorism are all forms of public violence.

Chapter 1

Forms of Public Violence

You probably hear about violence, which is words or actions that hurt people or the things they care about. Sometimes you might feel that violence is out of control. The good news is that violent crime has been decreasing in both Canada and the United States. Violence does happen, but you don't have to feel afraid all the time. You can learn to be careful and protect yourself. This book helps you to do that.

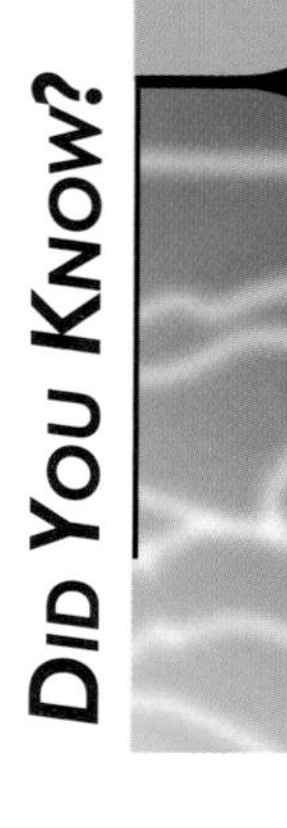

In the 1920s, Prohibition began in the United States. Prohibition was a law that said making, buying, or selling alcohol were crimes. Many people illegally made and sold alcohol. This helped lead to the growth of organized crime and public violence like drive-by shootings.

What Is a Public Place?

To talk about public violence, it helps to define a public place. A public place is a location where groups of people legally and freely can gather. Government buildings, museums, schools, or theaters are public places. Outdoor areas like streets, parks, or parking lots are public places, too. Land that someone privately owns or homes or apartments are not public places. Violence may occur in these areas, but this book describes violence only in public places.

Diedre, Age 17

Diedre and her family spent the day at the park. It was perfect. However, when the family returned to their car, they saw that someone had scratched letters into its paint. The scratches weren't large but would be expensive to fix. The damage changed the way Diedre felt about the day. Instead of feeling happy, she now felt angry and a little scared.

Vandalism

The word *violence* may bring to mind physical harm. However, violence is actions that hurt not only people but also the things people care about. Intentional harm to property is vandalism. Graffiti, or drawing or writing on a public surface, is a common example of vandalism. Scratching Diedre's family's car also was vandalism. Some drive-by shootings are vandalism. For example, gunfire may damage street signs or roadside mailboxes.

Although vandalism may not physically harm someone, it can deeply affect people emotionally. For example, the paint scratches didn't physically harm Diedre's family but did harm their property. The vandalism affected the way the family felt. They might feel less safe after the incident. They might be worried something similar might happen in the future.

Words as Violence

Violence is also words that hurt people. This verbal violence occurs more often in public places than physical violence does. For example, a group may make sexual comments to a young woman passing by. They do not touch or make a move toward her. However, she may be frightened. The words may have affected the way she feels. They are an act of violence against her.

Shouting angrily at someone on the street is another example of words used as violence. The people being shouted at are affected. Anyone else who sees or hears the people also might be affected.

Physical Violence

Many violent acts in public places are physical. Some examples of this are shoving someone while in line or bullying. Many people experience these sorts of things in their life. You may have experienced them or seen them happen.

Some kinds of violence in public places may result in physical injury. Examples of this kind of violence are robbery, assault, reckless manslaughter, random public violence, hate crimes, and terrorism.

"I never got so much respect as when I first pointed a gun at somebody. But, man, I sure paid the price when I pulled the trigger."—Al, age 19, jailed for armed robbery

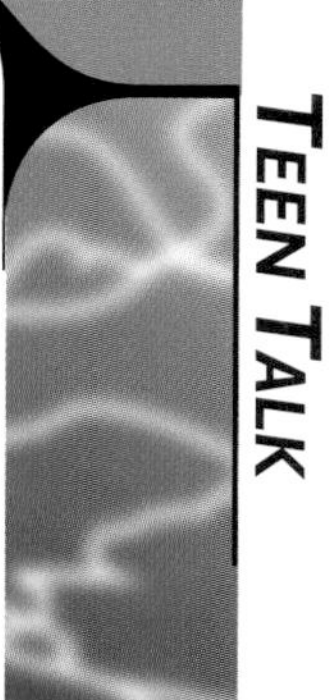

Robbery

Robbery in public places usually occurs as purse snatching, mugging, or holdups. Often, victims of robbery are hurt only if they try to resist the robber. Occasionally, robbery can lead to injury or death.

Experts have found that many people commit robbery not for money or possessions. They do it for power and the feeling of control they may not otherwise get.

Assault

Assault includes a threat or an attempt to harm someone physically. During 1998, Canadian police recorded about 225,000 assaults while U.S. police recorded about 975,000. Many of these assaults occurred in public places. The reason for most assaults in public is robbery. Some assaults have been related to gang activity or drug trafficking, which is buying or selling drugs. A drive-by shooting in which no one is killed is an example of assault.

Reckless Manslaughter

Some public violence occurs as a result of carelessness, alcohol or other drug use, or high-speed car crashes. This kind of accidental killing is called reckless manslaughter. For instance, many drunk drivers have killed people who were walking or were in other cars. People who are trying to get away from police may accidentally kill innocent people. People found guilty of reckless manslaughter might face a prison sentence even though they killed someone by accident.

Random Public Violence

Busy public places occasionally become the scene of random violence. This type of violence often has no order or reason. Most victims of random attacks don't know and haven't done anything to the attacker. They are simply in the wrong place at the wrong time. Sometimes the attacker is an angry person with mental illness. This seems to be the case in some of the following events from the late 1990s.

In July 1996, a bomb exploded at the Olympic Games in Atlanta. Two people died as a result of the blast. The reason for the bombing still is not completely clear.

In September 1997, a man pushed a young woman in front of a moving subway train in Toronto. She died in the hospital nine days later. The man didn't know the woman.

In August 1998, a man shot and killed one tourist and two security guards at the U.S. Capitol in Washington.

In November 1998, a man started firing a gun on a crowded bus in Seattle. The driver lost control of the bus, which ran off a bridge. Two people died, including the bus driver.

These kinds of events are frightening but are probably the least common sort of violence in public places.

Hate Crimes

Hate crimes are a type of random violence. The attackers usually target their victims simply for belonging to a particular group. Minority groups, immigrant groups from other countries, or religious groups are common targets of hate crimes. Women and people with certain sexual orientations also may be targets. Sexual orientation is sexual attraction, behavior, or desire for other people based on their gender.

Hate crimes usually occur in public places. For example, someone walking along the street may be called racist names. Graves in a cemetery may be vandalized because they represent a certain religion. Hate crimes sometimes include beatings and killings.

The U.S. and Canadian governments keep a close eye on hate crimes. So do nongovernment groups that protect the rights of minorities and monitor the activities of hate groups. Hate speech may be protected by law. Hate crimes aren't.

Terrorism

Terrorism is extreme violence that is intended to frighten people into doing what a group or individual wants. Terrorism has occurred worldwide but has been rare in the United States and Canada. Recently, however, there have been several terrorist attacks in the United States. In 1993, a terrorist bomb exploded beneath New York's World Trade Center. Five people were killed and hundreds were injured. In 1995, a truck bomb destroyed the Murrah Federal Building in Oklahoma City. The bomb killed 168 people, including 19 children.

Points to Consider

How would you feel if you saw an act of public violence?

How do you feel when you see graffiti or other vandalism?

Have you ever heard words used as violence? If so, how did you feel?

Which do you think is worst: robbery, assault, reckless manslaughter, random public violence, hate crimes, or terrorism? Explain.

Chapter Overview

Anger can bring about conditions that may lead to violence in public places. Lack of impulse control is another factor in violence.

Many abusers of children were abused as children. Abused children may grow up to commit violence in public.

The abuse of alcohol and other drugs contributes to many acts of public violence.

Part of the increase in violence can be linked to the availability of guns.

Media violence and road rage may contribute to public acts of violence.

Chapter 2
The Causes of Public Violence

The best way to deal with violence in public places is to stop it before it happens. To prevent violence, it's helpful to recognize some of its causes. It may be rooted in anger and lack of impulse control. Many experts believe that family problems are a cause. Others believe that alcohol and other drug abuse leads to public violence. Some people believe that violence in the media, such as TV, news, movies, or video games, contributes to violent behavior. The availability of guns also has been given as a cause of violence. Violence in public places likely comes from a combination of any of these things.

Anger

Anger powerfully influences people. It can be positive. For example, it can warn you of problems. It can help protect you from danger. It can be useful in changing unjust situations. For example, when a drunk driver killed two students, their angry classmates began Students Against Destructive Decisions (SADD).

Anger can be negative, too. It may lead people to lash out impulsively. If it is uncontrolled, it may lead to violence in public places.

Many things can trigger people's anger. For example, people may be teased or punched. They may be blocked from reaching a goal. They may feel that an act or situation is unfair or threatens someone's rights. Some people might feel angry because they believe that their life won't improve. People who feel powerless may see acting violently as the only way to change things.

By managing their anger, people are less likely to use violent actions. They will be better able to control their violent words, too.

Here is a four-step method for controlling anger:

1. **Admit you're angry.** A tense body or angry thoughts can tell you that you are angry.

2. **Calm down.** Don't strike out when you are angry. Instead, breathe deeply or count to 10 before responding. Exercising or doing a hobby can help you calm down, too.

3. **Think about your options.** Think of only nonviolent solutions, including not responding at all to the person or situation.

4. **Choose a solution and act on it.** If the solution doesn't work, go back to Step 3.

AT A GLANCE

BRAD, AGE 16

Brad was in line with some friends at the movie theater. Someone bumped him from behind. Brad spun around to see who had bumped him. "Sorry, man," said the guy. Brad decided the guy had bumped him on purpose. Instead of shrugging it off, Brad's first thought was to get even. "Yeah, you're gonna be sorry, all right," he said, shoving the guy hard in return.

Impulse Control

Part of growing up is learning self-control. For example, children must be taught to wait or share instead of grabbing everything they want. They learn not to hit or hurt others. Even teens still are learning to control their impulses. They may have more outbursts than adults as they learn to manage anger. When people have trouble controlling their impulses, one result can be violence in public places. Such violence often occurs because someone acts before thinking through the situation.

FAST FACT

Child abuse results in up to 5,000 deaths and 150,000 serious injuries each year in the United States.

Child Abuse and Public Violence

Pressures at work or in daily life may lead adults to abuse children physically or emotionally. Being abused can lead children to feel powerless and angry. Children who are abused also are likely to grow up believing that such violent behavior is acceptable. If children can't manage and resolve their anger, they sometimes act it out as public violence.

Abuse of Alcohol and Other Drugs

Alcohol and other drugs affect the normal working of the central nervous system. They make it difficult to think clearly. Abuse of alcohol and other drugs may encourage people to do things they normally might not do. Drug abuse includes any use of illegal drugs. It also includes using legal drugs and medicines in a way they were not meant to be used. Abuse includes using other substances such as glue or gasoline in ways they were not intended.

"When I was 12, my sister Mary gave me a joint. I started using marijuana all the time after that. I never seemed to have enough money to get more, so I began shoplifting. I'd sell the stuff I stole, but I didn't get enough money that way, either. When I broke into an electronics store, I got arrested and ended up in jail. Mary's sorry she gave me that first joint, but it's not her fault. I'm the one who took that first drag. I'm just glad I was stopped before I hurt someone to get money."—Mike, age 17

TEEN TALK

The lack of control that alcohol and other drug abuse triggers may cause violence in public. For example, a drunk driver may hit someone on the sidewalk or crash into another car.

Experimenting with drugs can lead to addiction. This occurs when the body needs more and more of a drug to feel good. Addiction can lead to violent crime when drug users need money for more drugs. Public violence such as shoplifting, robbery, or assault are common ways for people to get money for drugs.

Many people are involved in drug trafficking. This is among the most dangerous activities on the street. Drug traffickers are at high risk to be treated violently. Gang involvement in drug traffic increases violence in public, especially if rivalries for drug trade develop.

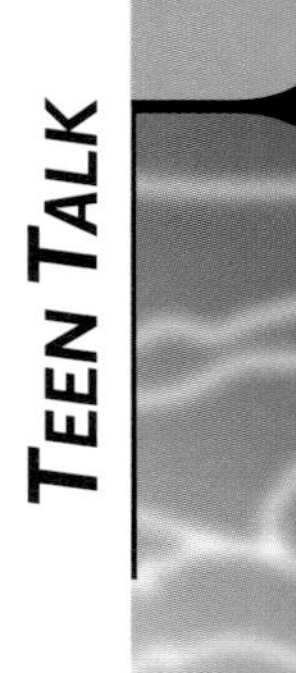

"A kid named Dan was pushing me around. One time I got my grandpa's gun from home. I went looking for Dan. I was thinking, 'He's gonna get it.' I'm just glad I didn't find him until I had cooled down. By then I felt calmer."—Jack, age 15

Availability of Guns

An estimated 60 percent of teens say that they could get a handgun if they wanted one. Many homes have guns that belong to parents or other adults who share the house. When guns are readily available to people who don't control their impulses, violence is more likely to happen. The physical harm that may occur also is likely to be more serious.

Media Violence

Violence shown in the media hasn't been proved to cause real-life violence. However, research has shown that media violence strongly influences young people who already live with violence in their life. They may constantly feel ready for "fight or flight." The violence that appears in the media increases this feeling of tenseness and fear. Media violence is likely to influence these young people more than others to commit their own public violence.

For instance, point-and-shoot video games alone don't cause violence. However, they can influence players to be less sensitive to harming others. They also can increase a player's accuracy. For years, the U.S. military has used video games to teach soldiers how to kill better in war. In at least one U.S. school shooting, the shooter's accuracy was increased because of practice with such games.

Road Rage

People sometimes are injured or killed because of violent activity on public highways. As streets and freeways become more crowded, people seem to be less patient with one another. Such crowding, or congestion, may lead to aggressive behavior while driving, which is sometimes called road rage.

Road rage can include shouting at other drivers, driving dangerously, and using weapons. Another person's discourteous driving may trigger the rage. Events outside the driver's control may trigger it. For example, a driver may be late to work as a result of being in a traffic jam. The driver may become impatient. When some people become impatient, they are likely to react angrily to the situation. This is another example of people's lack of impulse control.

Experts believe that people who drive cooperatively receive cooperation from other drivers in return. Aggressive driving, however, may trigger others' instinct to fight back.

Political Violence

Individuals or groups with strong political ideas sometimes cause violence in public places. The violence may be against property. For example, logging equipment has been wrecked to keep trees from being cut down and used for lumber or paper. Some groups are against using animal fur for clothing. They have splashed blood or paint on the fur coats of people with different views. Sometimes people physically harm other people to stop their actions. For example, some doctors who help women end their pregnancy have been injured and even killed.

Points to Consider

How do you control your anger? Explain.

Do you think alcohol abuse is as serious as the abuse of other drugs? Explain.

How might stricter gun control help stop violence?

Do you think that violence in the media influences real-life violence? Explain.

Have you ever felt another driver's anger while you were in a car? What happened?

Chapter Overview

Victims of violence may have physical and emotional pain. Some victims even may die.

The families and friends of victims may have serious emotional scars. Witnesses of violence in public may have emotional effects.

Compassion fatigue makes people less able to help others.

Fear of violence in public can lead to a negative cycle of feelings and behavior.

Violence has financial and emotional costs.

Chapter 3

The Effects of Public Violence

You may read or hear about violent events on TV or in the news. Maybe you even fear becoming a victim of violence. Many people have an increased fear for their friends and loved ones. In a survey, 60 percent of Americans said they felt very worried about their personal safety. Public violence can affect many people including those who were not directly involved. It can affect the victims, their family and friends, witnesses, and the general public.

Effects on Victims

The victim of a robbery, drive-by shooting, random violence, or an assault has the most obvious effects. For example, the person may need care at a hospital or physical therapy to recover. Some victims die from their injuries.

Myth: Violent crime is increasing.

Fact: Canadian and U.S. government figures show that violent crime has decreased since 1993. In 1998, U.S. crime rates were at their lowest levels in 15 years.

The emotional effects that public violence creates can cause physical symptoms in victims. For example, victims may be unable to sleep or concentrate. They may have constant headaches, back problems, or stomachaches. They may become angry with other people for no apparent reason. They may be unable to eat or may eat too much.

Along with the physical symptoms, victims also can have deep emotional effects. For example, a person whose house is vandalized with hate messages may become afraid to go out in public. The person even may become afraid to be alone at home. The person may require counseling to get over the fear and anger. Sometimes, the victim may not be ready to relive the experience by talking about it. At other times, the victim may need to talk about what happened. When ready, a victim can benefit from talking with a friend, family member, or professional counselor.

Some people become so frightened that they feel a need to carry a weapon such as a gun. Most people who carry a gun say they do it for self-protection. However, the more guns people have, the greater the chance that someone will get hurt. The reality is that carrying a weapon doesn't make people safer.

Effects on Loved Ones

The harm to victims of violence often is easy to see. However, the harm to family members and friends may not be so obvious. For example, people who witness harm to a loved one have to live with emotional scars resulting from the violence. They have to heal from the pain of watching a loved one suffer. If a loved one is killed, the grief of the families and friends is overwhelming.

Sometimes the family members suffer so much that they are unable to help the victim. If this happens, they may need counseling to deal with their feelings about what has occurred. Many agencies offer help to loved ones of victims of violence.

Effects on Witnesses

An act of violence in a public place may deeply affect witnesses. Particularly brutal violence can cause trauma in the person who sees it. This type of severe physical or emotional shock may overwhelm the witness's sense of control, connection, and meaning in life. The witness may feel afraid, alone, or helpless. A witness who sees someone die as a result of violence may have double trauma. The person must deal with both the violence that caused the death and the death itself.

Like victims and their loved ones, witnesses may need counseling to get over the shock they feel. They might want to talk with an understanding friend or may need to see a professional counselor.

Dealing with the effects of violent crime costs the United States more than $400 billion a year. That is four times more than one year's cost of funding all criminal justice agencies and activities.

FAST FACT

Effects on Professionals

Some social workers have suggested the idea that people surrounded by violence may have compassion fatigue. This is a feeling of being tired and depressed. Compassion fatigue is sometimes called burnout. It occasionally happens to people in such helping professions as counseling. These people may have the feeling that they can't do anything to help. This may lessen their ability to care about other people's problems.

Fear and Public Violence

Fear can seriously change the mood of a public setting. If people are afraid to be in certain public areas, they will begin to avoid the areas. Violence or crime may increase in these areas because fewer people are around. For example, some big cities are struggling economically because people avoid them out of fear. People may even feel they must move somewhere else to be safe.

Sometimes people's fear of violence leads to mistrust and aggression toward others. This behavior can lead to a negative cycle of fear and violence. In this cycle, others in turn behave aggressively.

Growing Costs

Everyone pays for violence in public. An increasing amount of time, energy, and money is devoted to dealing with public violence. Police salaries, court costs, and prison construction and repair are a few examples of financial costs.

An emotional cost of public violence is decreasing trust that people have for each other. Another cost is a decreasing sense of community among people.

Points to Consider

How could you help a victim or witness of public violence?

Have you ever avoided a public place because you were afraid? If so, what happened?

Do you think you could help counter the fear that comes with violence in a public place? Why or why not?

Chapter Overview

Strong, loving families are important in helping children become violence-free adults.

Help is available for families in raising their children.

Changes in the criminal justice system might decrease the number of repeat offenses.

Curbing alcohol and other drug abuse and drug trafficking can reduce crime.

Gun control laws can reduce the amount of violent crime. The Brady Bill requires a waiting period for gun sales. Assault weapons were outlawed in 1994. Every state has passed or is working on gun control laws.

Chapter 4
Preventing Public Violence

People have many ideas about how to prevent violence in public places. The best ideas focus on reaching children. Kids who learn how to be nonviolent usually grow up better able to control themselves.

"I think that people who don't *really* have the time, energy, or interest in caring for children should choose not to be parents."—Carrie, age 17

Carter, Age 16

Carter is 16. His neighbor, Ben, has been like a father or big brother to him. Ben has always cared about how Carter is doing in school and at home. Ben has helped Carter be respectful of other people. He has taught Carter about right and wrong. He has always listened to Carter. Ben has given a sense of how important Carter is. Carter feels he can do almost anything he sets out to do.

Strong, Loving Adults

It's a big job for adults who have or care for children to devote themselves to taking care of those children. Whether a parent, a grandparent, or another guardian, a caregiver has a major responsibility. To grow into a violence-free individual, it's helpful for a young person to have at least one caring adult's attention. Sometimes teachers, coaches, or other people can give children that attention if parents or guardians don't. These caring adults may even be able to make up for a certain degree of neglect. Children who don't get needed attention often feel only like a bother to the adults in their life.

Many authorities believe that good parenting is the most important way to reduce crime. If a child does not feel cared for and guided, he or she may not care for others. The child may not know or care about leading a moral life. Sometimes this lack of love and security causes children to grow into angry teens and adults. This anger can cause aggressive behavior toward others. Studies show that children who feel unwanted are more likely to abuse alcohol and other drugs.

Help for Families

Many communities have professional people who help families raise children. Programs such as Hawaii's Healthy Start begin during pregnancy. They help a family through a child's first year of life. The services range from dealing with childhood illness to finding a job for parents. Test groups have found fewer cases of child abuse in the families that these programs help.

Another program that helps families is the Yale Child Welfare Research Program. It aids single mothers during pregnancy. It also provides preschool guidance for children in learning to play well with others. This program, too, has positively affected children. It has helped them learn to handle their feelings in a healthy manner.

Sometimes having a job can help a person avoid violence. The Job Corps is one of the oldest job skills training programs for young people. Participation in the Job Corps has greatly reduced violence among its graduates.

The Quantum Opportunity Program is related to the Job Corps. Its students receive regular training in high-tech jobs all during high school. The program involves students in community service. It matches them with long-term mentors, who are available to help and guide the students. It also encourages students' attendance at theater, music, and other cultural events.

About 7 out of 10 Americans feel people under age 18 should be treated as adults in court.

FAST FACT

Punishment and Rehabilitation

Punishment for violent crime has long been discussed in every society. Often punishments have been harsh. Such punishment was meant to keep others from committing a similar crime. Authorities often made no effort to rehabilitate offenders, or help them get back into society.

Many authorities believe that putting such young offenders in prison and isolating them from society doesn't work. A different approach to preventing crime does not punish young offenders. Instead, it involves keeping them from repeatedly breaking the law. For rehabilitation to succeed, young offenders must learn to deal with family, friends, school, and work. For example, Missouri's Juvenile Court Diversion Project places less serious offenders in counseling. This lets them avoid court and instead learn how to take charge of their life. Such programs have proved successful in preventing repeat crime, including public violence.

Alcohol and Other Drug Abuse

Many people feel that reducing illegal drug use and trafficking can help decrease public violence.

Governments can help control the availability of alcohol. City governments can restrict where liquor stores may operate. State and provincial governments can enforce a minimum legal drinking age. The federal government can limit the advertising of alcoholic beverages. If the amount of drinking among young people is lowered, the number of injuries and deaths from drunk driving may drop. The number of deaths and injuries from other public violence also may drop.

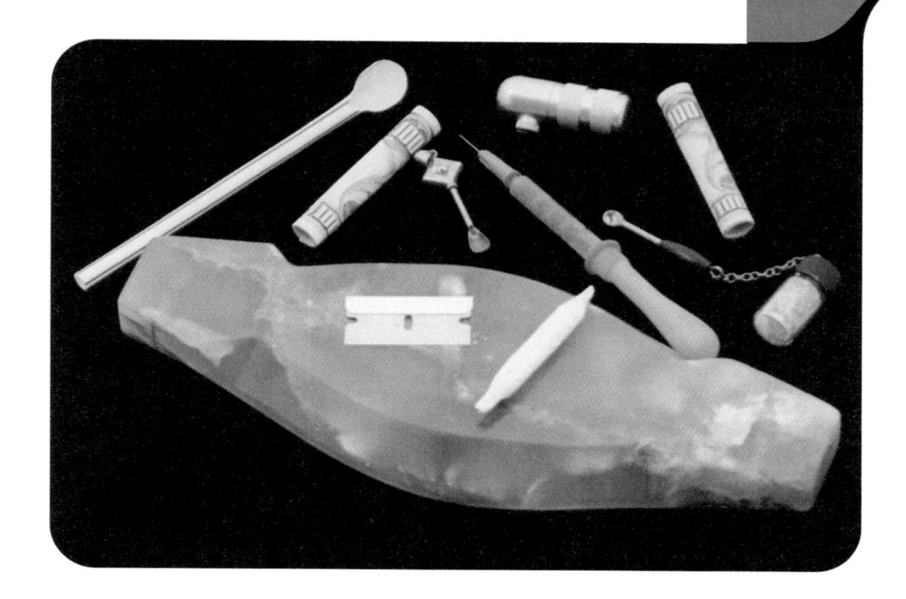

Many steps are being taken to reduce illegal drug use. For example, the U.S. and Canadian governments make ongoing efforts to reduce the flow of drugs into the country. Education about drugs is important. Teens need to know about the specific effects of drugs. They also need to learn ways to refuse drugs. Treatment programs offer help to teens who have become addicted.

At a Glance

In Canada, only members of approved target shooting clubs, collectors, and some security guards may legally own guns. Canadians own 1 million handguns and 6 million rifles. The U.S. Bureau of Alcohol, Tobacco, and Firearms estimates that Americans own 223 million firearms, including more than 75 million handguns.

Gun Control

Gun control may be another way to prevent public violence. Thousands of people in the United States die each year in gun-related accidents, murders, and suicides. Many of these shootings occur in public places.

The availability of guns is related to increased crime and death. The more guns people carry, the more likely it is that deadly accidents and intentional violence will occur. One way to reduce such violence is with stricter gun controls.

In recent years, many efforts have been made to control guns and the damage they can do. Several gun control laws have been passed. For example, the Brady Bill is one such law in the United States passed in 1993. The law requires a waiting period for people who apply to buy a handgun. During the waiting period, a buyer's criminal record can be checked. The U.S. Department of Justice estimates that the Brady Bill stopped more than 173,000 criminals from buying handguns in 1997.

A ban on selling or owning assault weapons was passed in the United States in 1994. Assault weapons are military-style rifles. Hunters or most people seeking protection do not use assault weapons. Sometimes people or groups trying to harm the most people in the shortest time have used these weapons. The weapons also have been used in gang wars.

One out of four state groups surveyed reported action on new gun laws or regulations. All of these laws are either new since 1995 or are in the process of being passed. Eighty percent of citizens surveyed believe guns should be sold only by or to licensed firearms dealers.

Points to Consider

Do you think it is important to have adults in your life who care about you? Why or why not?

Do you think teen offenders should be tried as adults? Why or why not?

What is the most important thing that could be done to prevent violence in public places? Explain.

Chapter Overview

Awareness of your surroundings is important to remaining safe in public. Trusting your instincts about a person or a place is another good tool in keeping yourself safe. If you don't feel safe, trust that feeling.

To avoid violence in a public place, it always helps to think ahead. There are many ways to do this.

When you avoid behaving in a stereotyped way, you can help to keep yourself safer.

Chapter 5

Protecting Yourself in Public Places

Becoming Aware

Sometimes people take for granted that public places are safe. However, violence can occur anywhere people gather. This does not mean that you must live in fear of being assaulted or robbed. You don't have to stay home because someone's words may be violent. However, it is a good idea to pay attention to what is going on around you. Be aware of where you are and who is around you. This helps you to take care of yourself. Paying attention to your surroundings is something you can practice and learn to do naturally.

SHALIKA, AGE 16

One day after school, Shalika and Barb were walking home from school. Barb was talking nonstop as usual. Shalika was listening, but she also was keeping an eye on the neighborhood. This wasn't the best street. There were a lot of places for people to hide, and no one else was on the street.

Suddenly Shalika stopped walking and Barb stopped talking. Shalika saw five older boys standing ahead on the sidewalk. They were staring and pointing at Shalika and Barb. "Let's cross the street," said Shalika. Barb answered, "They aren't going to do anything. It's broad daylight." "Maybe, but it just doesn't feel right," said Shalika. She pulled Barb off to the side and then across the street. The boys followed.

The girls walked faster, then ran for almost two blocks to a convenience store. The boys approached the store but stopped down the street. The girls told the store clerk what had happened. The clerk called the police, who arrived in minutes. The boys ran off. The police gave Shalika and Barb a ride home. Shalika was glad she had trusted her instincts.

If you witness a violent act in public, call 9-1-1. Don't get involved yourself. Let the police handle the situation.

DID YOU KNOW?

Like your awareness of the surroundings, your instincts are also a valuable tool for self-protection. If a certain person, place, or situation scares you, there may be a good reason. If you feel something isn't right, it probably isn't. Trust that feeling. It is better to be safe than sorry. For example, Shalika trusted her instincts about the boys, even though she could see nothing wrong.

What You Can Do

It is not likely that you will experience violence in a public place. However, it is always wise to think ahead about how you can protect yourself and others. Here are some things you can do.

Avoid people who behave suspiciously. Trust your instincts, even if you aren't sure what's wrong.

Be aware of the people around you. This is especially important if you are far from help or if you are carrying money.

Use familiar routes when walking or exercising. Walk in places that you know are safe, well lighted, and used by many people.

Don't get too involved with portable music. Headphones might keep you from hearing possible dangers around you.

Carry your most important valuables in a pocket, not in a purse or backpack.

Use automatic teller machines and pay phones that are inside well-lighted places with other people around.

Be polite to others if you drive.

Remain calm if you find yourself in a potentially violent situation.

If by remote chance you are attacked, scream unless the attacker threatens you with a weapon.

The U.S. National Highway Traffic Safety Administration recommends these tips for dealing with others' road rage:

Don't take traffic problems personally.

Avoid looking aggressive drivers in the eye.

Don't make angry gestures at other drivers.

Don't drive too closely behind others.

Don't honk or flash your lights at people who drive aggressively.

Stay away from cars with aggressive drivers. Get their license number and report them to the police when you safely can.

AT A GLANCE

Avoiding Stereotypes

Stereotypes are overly simple ideas about people. They allow entire groups to be treated unfairly without any thought. By acting in ways that don't agree with stereotypes, you may be able to avoid public violence.

One stereotype about females is that they are easy victims. However, just being female does not make a person an easy victim. If you are female, look confident and make eye contact. Someone may think twice about making a violent comment or gesture. If you are attacked, your sudden scream or kick may not seem ladylike. However, it may get you out of a dangerous situation. Don't let ideas about what females do or don't do put you in danger.

One common stereotype about males is that they should not allow themselves to be victims. However, just being male does not make a person safe from violence in public. If you are male, don't be careless because you think you won't encounter violence. Don't act macho or get in a fight over money or personal belongings. Macho behavior can cause a situation to become more violent. For example, an attacker may have a weapon and decide to use it if you fight back. Even if no weapon is present, a person who wants something from you may have help to get it. Just because you are male doesn't mean that you can't yell for help or even run away. It is important not to let ideas about how males should or shouldn't behave put you in danger.

Points to Consider

Do you agree that staying aware of your surroundings is a good idea? Why or why not?

What might you do if you were attacked while jogging?

How might listening to music on headphones put you in danger?

How might traditional ideas about males and females put someone in danger?

Chapter Overview

Programs to curb drug abuse and drug trafficking are being started in many places. They have successfully reduced violence in public.

The U.S. rate for seven serious crimes reached its lowest point in 15 years. Canada had its lowest number of murders since 1973. This downward trend is good news.

Individual teens can do many things to help oppose violence at school and in the community.

Chapter 6

Moving Ahead

Some people feel that violence in public places is out of control. However, many actions have been taken to reduce such violence. Governments and independent organizations have begun initiatives to reduce the number of guns. City groups have successfully reduced violent public crimes. Individuals like you also can act to help to stop public violence at school and in the community.

DID YOU KNOW?

The Brady Bill is named for James Brady, the press secretary for former President Ronald Reagan. President Reagan was shot on a street in Washington, D.C., in 1981. Brady received a wound in the head during the shooting. The wound partially paralyzed Brady. Since then, Brady and his wife, Sarah, have worked for stricter gun controls in the United States.

Continuing Gun Control Efforts

Every state in America is moving to reduce gun violence. Join Together, a group that opposes gun violence, has surveyed state groups. Join Together has found 10 states with more than a dozen groups in them that oppose gun violence. California has 30 of these groups. That is the most for any one state.

Cities and individuals have begun to take action, too. Some groups have taken gun manufacturers to court. They hope to make manufacturers accountable for the effects of the gun violence. For example, in early 1999, seven families of shooting victims sued 25 manufacturers in a Brooklyn court. The jury found 15 of the gun manufacturers guilty of poor gun-selling practices. The jury seemed to feel that the companies had allowed guns to fall into the wrong hands.

Successes in Reducing Drug-Related Violence in Public

City groups have taken steps toward reducing the public violence that comes with drug trafficking. For example, the Miami Coalition recently persuaded authorities to demolish more than 2,000 known crack houses. These are abandoned buildings where drugs are sold or used. As a result, drug use has decreased by 40 percent and crime by 24 percent.

The Safe Streets Campaign in Tacoma, Washington, has involved 8,000 community members, including 2,000 teens. They have removed graffiti, closed 600 drug markets, and reduced 9-1-1 calls by 23,000 per year.

San Antonio Fighting Back has formed a partnership between police and community members. The goal is to fight crime and drugs. Burglaries have decreased by 19 percent and auto theft by 23 percent. The partnership has closed 85 crack houses.

A Wonderful Trend

The overall rate of violent crime in the United States peaked in 1993. Since then, the rates for seven serious crimes have been falling. These crimes are robbery, murder, rape, assault, burglary, theft, and car theft. In 1998, the rates reached their lowest point in 15 years. Murder and robbery were at their lowest point in 30 years.

In Canada, rates for murder and robbery have been falling since 1991. Both the U.S. and Canadian rates are predicted to keep dropping, continuing the trend of decreasing public violence.

Teens Reducing Violence

Teens can help reduce violence in public places. You probably can think of many ways to help reduce public violence where you live. Here are a few ideas for your school and your community.

At School

Learn when not to keep quiet. If you hear plans being made for violent actions, report them to a teacher or another trusted adult. Knowing when not to keep quiet is part of keeping yourself and others safe.

Work with teachers and counselors. Develop a safe way to report bullying, threats, weapons, drugs, gang activity, or vandalism.

Start or join a peer mediation group. People usually react better when they help control what happens to them.

Become a peer counselor to help classmates who need support.

Help organize a school assembly to talk about peaceful compromise.

Fast Fact

Do Something, a community-based organization, reports that in the last year, one-third of people ages 15 to 29 have volunteered for community service. Volunteers are important in easing conditions that encourage public violence.

Introduce new students to your friends and other people you know. Everyone needs someone who cares about them.

Start a school crime watch to help keep an eye on hallways and parking lots.

Start a peace pledge campaign. In such a campaign, students promise to work out disagreements without using violence.

Be a mentor or role model for a younger student.

In the Community

Get to know your neighbors. This helps build a sense of safety. It also helps you and the neighbors know when people from outside the neighborhood are present.

Organize neighborhood walks. Neighborhood volunteers take turns patrolling the neighborhood. The presence of people is a good way to prevent crime.

Tell people that you think violence is not acceptable.

Organize and attend block parties for your neighborhood.

Suggest nonviolent ways to solve problems. For example, work out your arguments or walk away from them.

Avoid racism, sexism, and other types of prejudice. This gives people basic respect.

Work with the community to create new and better activities for young children. For example, after-school and weekend programs help people feel connected.

Invite friends and family members to join you in writing to legislators about stricter gun control laws. Lawmakers do listen when the people they represent say what they think.

Volunteer at a local community service agency.

Don't carry a weapon.

Angelista, Age 16

Angelista loves children, but she doesn't want her own for several years. Instead, she has decided to volunteer at Happy Hands. This free daycare center is for single parents who have to work. Angelista works there for three hours twice a week.

Each day at Happy Hands Angelista reads to the children. She plays games with them. She helps teach them to share toys.

Angelista has met many parents of the kids in the center. She sees their joy because they know their children are being well cared for. Angelista doesn't make any money doing this work. She knows, however, that her work is important.

Points to Consider

How do you feel about gun control? Explain.

Why do you think U.S. and Canadian violent crime rates have dropped?

How do you think volunteer work can help reduce violent crime in public places?

Glossary

addiction (uh-DIK-shuhn)—the condition in which the body needs more and more of a drug to feel good

assault (uh-SAWLT)—a threat or an attempt to harm someone physically

assault weapon (uh-SAWLT WEP-uhn)—military-style rifle

coalition (koh-uh-LISH-uhn)—two or more groups joined together for a common purpose

crack (KRAK)—a highly addictive, smokable form of the illegal drug cocaine

graffiti (gruh-FEE-tee)—illegal drawing or writing on a public surface

public place (PUHB-lik PLAYSS)—anywhere people can gather legally and freely

random (RAN-duhm)—without any order or purpose

reckless manslaughter (RECK-liss MAN-slaw-tur)—the accidental killing of someone through carelessness

rehabilitate (ree-huhb-IL-uh-tayt)—to help someone become a productive member of society

road rage (ROHD RAYJ)—aggressive, angry behavior while driving

trauma (TRAW-muh)—a severe and painful emotional shock or physical injury

vandalism (VAN-duhl-izm)—needless destruction of or damage to other people's property

violence (VYE-uh-luhnss)—words or actions that hurt people or the things they care about

For More Information

Dosick, Wayne. *Golden Rules.* San Francisco: Harper San Francisco, 1995.

Gedatus, Gus. *Gangs and Violence.* Mankato, MN: Capstone, 2000.

Gedatus, Gus. *Violence at School.* Mankato, MN: Capstone, 2000.

Mizell, Louis, Jr. *Street Sense for Women: Staying Safe in a Violent World.* New York: Berkley, 1995.

Peacock, Judith. *Anger Management.* Mankato, MN: Capstone, 2000.

Useful Addresses and Internet Sites

Center for Conflict Resolution
200 North Michigan Avenue, Suite 500
Chicago, IL 60601

Center to Prevent Handgun Violence
1225 I Street Northwest
Suite 1100
Washington, DC 20005
www.cphv.org

National Crime Prevention Council
1700 K Street, Second floor
Washington, DC 20006
www.ncpc.org

American Psychological Society
http://helping.apa.org/warningsigns/index.html
Facts and information about violence

Join Together Online
www.jointogether.org/gv
Information and facts about guns, gun violence, and gun control in the United States

Media Campaign
www.mediacampaign.org
Links to sites with information about drugs and other issues

U.S. Department of Justice
Justice for Kids and Youth
www.usdoj.gov/kidspage
Ideas on fighting crime, hate, and injustice

Index

Index continued